CW00401303

Dedication

To Morgan, my Right Hand Cat

And these wonderful artists

butter fly

First Published 2022

Text, Characters and Illustrations © James Pluckrose

All Rights Reserved

The Moral right of the creator has been asserted

ISBN - 9798351295787 -

Alice Anderson

A Mountain Walk

Alice and her Family are spending this week with Nanny and Grandad.

Alice has to share her room with Adam, her younger brother.

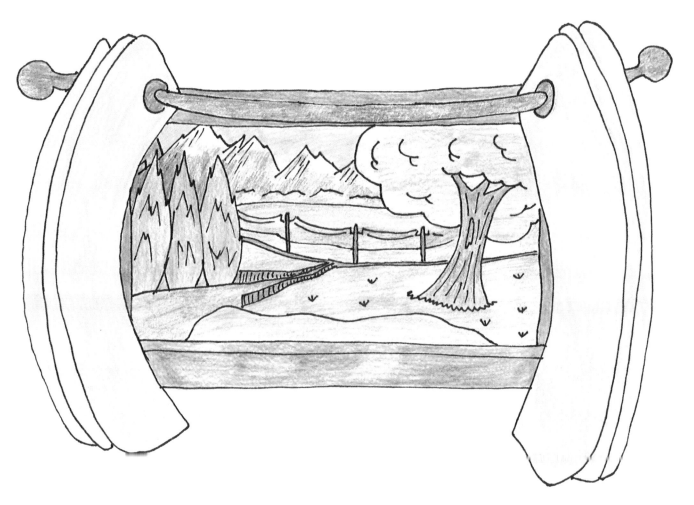

When Mummy opens the curtains, they can see a special lake called a Loch.

"Nanny and Grandad say that a monster hides in the Loch" explained Alice as she peered through her binoculars, "But I haven't seen it yet."

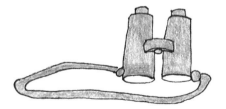

A Loch is the Scottish word for a lake. Loch Ness is a famous Loch, fabled to be home to the mysterious Nessie, an ancient Mystical creature.

Today they are going on a long walk to
the very top of a mountain.

Nanny and Grandad know the way, Mummy and
Daddy are making a picnic.

When it was ready, Daddy helped Alice put on her wellies.

(Not the easiest of jobs)

Then they all got into Grandad's big
old blue truck.

They drove to a large green field at the bottom
of a giant mountain.

It rose to the clouds and there was a
path that went all the way to the top.

The family had their picnic first,
Nanny and Grandad wished them
luck as they were staying at the
bottom.

Then they started their walk, they began by crossing over a wooden gate.

They walked on and passed
groups of fluffy sheep.

They walked more,

moving around giant boulders.

They kept walking.

and walking

and...

"This is tiring"
Alice grumbled.

They kept on walking passing by hundreds of colourful flowers.

16

They found a river with a little waterfall to have a rest.

"Come on, we are nearly there" encouraged Mummy

So they kept on walking.

and walking

until...

They had reached the very top.

"Phew" said everyone as they looked at the amazing view.

That was a very long walk. Luckily the trip back
down was much easier.

Printed by Amazon Italia Logistica S.r.l.
Torrazza Piemonte (TO), Italy

43650363R00018